Jim Benton's Tales from Mackerel Middle School

DEAR DUMB DIARY,

THE PROBLEM WITH HERE IS THAT IT'S WHERE I'M FROM

BY JAMIE KELLY

SCHOLASTIC INC.

New York   Toronto   London   Auckland   Sydney
Mexico City   New Delhi   Hong Kong   Buenos Aires

READ NO FURTHER

For the young artists and writers

Special thanks to Maria Barbo, Shannon Penney, Steve Scott, Kara Edwards, and Craig Walker. And thank you to the Scholastic Book Clubs and Scholastic Book Fairs for all their support.

ISBN-13: 978-0-439-79622-4
ISBN-10: 0-439-79622-9

12 11 10 9 8 7 6 5 4 3   7 8 9 10 11 12/0
Printed in the U.S.A.   40
First Scholastic Printing, July 2007

TOTALLY PRIVATE

This Diary Property of:

Jamie Kelly

SCHOOL: Mackerel Middle School

LOCKER: 101

Best friend: Isabella

Favorite place: Elsewhere

Favorite food: FOREIGN flavored

LOOK,

I'm not sure how they do things where **YOU'RE** from, but around **HERE,** people keep their BIG **FAT** *NOSES* out of other people's *BIDNESS*

Dear Whoever Is Reading My Dumb Diary,

Are you sure you're supposed to be reading somebody else's diary? Maybe I told you that you could, so that's okay. But if you are Angeline, or anybody else that gets everything the easy way, I did **NOT** give you permission, **SO STOP IT!**

If you are my parents, then **YES**, I know that I am not allowed to call people blond-wads or to spread rumors or make crank calls, but this is a diary, so maybe I didn't actually "do" any of these things. I *wrote* them. And, if you punish me for it, then I will know that you read my diary, which I am not giving you permission to do.

Now, by the power vested in me, I do promise that everything in this diary is true, or at least as true as I think it needs to be — although now that I think about it, I'm not really wearing a vest. . . .

Signed, *Jamie Kelly*

PS: You should know that I heard about this one girl, from another school or something, who read somebody's diary without permission. She felt so guilty about it that she could never smile again as long as she lived. Not even at koalas or when this blond girl she knew got a pimple the size of a pineapple right in the middle of her forehead.

PPS: Oh! And there was another kid I heard about who felt so guilty after he read somebody's diary that he lost his will to enjoy himself and watched only golf on TV for the rest of his life.

fatally BORED

Sunday 01

Dear Dumb Diary,

   I'm trying to grow an accent.
   Isabella was over last night and we were watching this movie and it had this one girl from England in it and everything she said sounded smart or dainty.
   She could say, "Oh, do pardon me, but my little pup has just dropped a major steamer on your priceless antique tablecloth. Frightfully sorry."
   And you probably wouldn't even be mad. You'd be all, "Oh, yes, well, my fault for putting a priceless antique tablecloth in my house where your dog might leave a dumpereeno."

Isabella says that people in other countries are born with strange mouth deformities that make them talk that way, and that we should consider ourselves lucky that we can speak normally.

I think she's wrong. (It *has* happened before.) I'm going to try to grow an accent anyway. Do you think people who talk with accents write with accents?

Isabella says she's heard Angeline speak Spanish or French or something. I'm sure she learned it in some sort of unfair easy way, like being born with the deformity Isabella correctly identified, and not through the rigorous study that I am enduring at the **University of Watching TV.**

MOUTH DEFORMITIES OF THE FOREIGN

BABABA

SOUNDS FUNNY EVEN WHEN DISCUSSING FUNERALS

ALWAYS SOUNDS LIKE THEY'RE CLEARING THEIR THROAT

CAN'T SAY "BANANA"

Monday 02

Dear Dumb Diary,

    Okay, I get it. Everybody always loves Angeline best. Is it just because she's tall and slim and blond? So is a **MOP**. You don't see anybody getting all lovey-dovey with one of those.

    Although in elementary school, I once saw a janitor doing something that still makes me uncomfortable around mops. To make a long story short: Janitors are people, too, and Valentine's Day can be a very lonely time.

Today they announced that later on this month, they would be handing out ballots so we can vote for people in categories like MOST ARTISTIC, FUNNIEST, and BEST FRIENDS.

Of course one of the categories is PRETTIEST, and I overheard some people at lunch going, "Why don't they just print Angeline's name on the ballot for PRETTIEST? Everybody knows she's going to win. She *always* wins."

This is *terribly* unrealistic, because if a train tragically crashed into Angeline's face, we'd have a whole bunch of useless ballots on our hands. And I'm not just thinking of myself here—the train owner would have a bunch of smushed gorgeousness to wipe off the front of the train.

BEAUTY REMOVER

COAL

Isabella always wins for **MOST CLEVER,** but she works really hard for that. And I always win for **MOST ARTISTIC,** and I work really hard for that, too—often exposing myself to sequin fumes for hours on end. But not Angeline. She wins **PRETTIEST** without even trying. It's just not fair that everything is so automatically easy for Angeline.

Seriously, isn't it time we took a stand against the **Effortlessly Beautiful?**

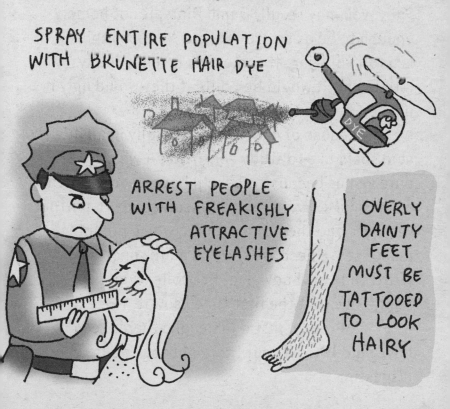

SPRAY ENTIRE POPULATION WITH BRUNETTE HAIR DYE

DYE

ARREST PEOPLE WITH FREAKISHLY ATTRACTIVE EYELASHES

OVERLY DAINTY FEET MUST BE TATTOOED TO LOOK HAIRY

Tuesday 03

Dear Dumb Diary,

Mr. Evans started us on another one of his famous projects today. He wants us to explore people and cultures through the different things they write. Then he asked us to throw ideas out there.

Sally, of course, immediately had ideas. Sally, you may recall, Dumb Diary, is not homely enough to be as smart as she is—which I think is a form of lying. If somebody is really really intelligent, it would be polite if they would ugly it up a bit before they left the house.

Because of her smartness, Sally immediately said she'd like to study song lyrics—which was pure genius because all she'll have to do is listen to music. Mr. Evans asked for somebody to partner with her, and then chose Anika, which probably makes sense because she has more songs on her **iPod** than anybody else. Her collection is so impressive that the first time I saw it, **iPeed.**

Not really. Just a little joke there. I could have said **iPood,** but I thought that would be too disgusting.

Margaret said she wanted to study poems, and Mr. Evans asked if anybody wanted to partner with her on that. Only **T.U.K.W.N.I.F.** (That Ugly Kid Whose Name I Forget) raised his hand, which would have horrified most girls, but Margaret totally smiled. Kind of romantic, right? Love is weird, because even though Margaret is sort of gross (chews pencils, burps super loud) and **T.U.K.W.N.I.F.** is sort of gross (dirty nails, lunch always smells like wet baloney), the fact that the two of them really have feelings for each other makes them somehow seem eleven times grosser.

CORN COBBERY

(I have to give Margaret a little credit here: Her beaverlike behavior has resulted in an ability to gnaw crude shapes out of pencils, which I guess makes her a sculptor, if anybody is looking for teensy, spitty totem poles.)

Of course, Angeline also thinks pretty fast on her feet because they are tiny and dainty and more like what podiatrists call hooves anyway. She said she'd like to study graffiti. (In case you don't know, Dumb Diary, graffiti is all the stuff people write on walls.) Dumb idea, huh? But here's the thing, I knew in **ONE SECOND** Mr. Evans was going to ask for a partner to volunteer, and in **TWO SECONDS** every hand in the room would go up. And Angeline — who has nothing but very easy triumphs — would triumph again, triumphantly. So, I dumbly did the only dumb thing I could dumbly do. **I took a stand.**

she probably ~~thinks~~ the whole world is her ice cream cone

And we're just the sprinkles that live on it

I blurted out, "Aww. I was going to say that!" And Evans did exactly what I knew he would do. **He paired us up.**

It all happened before I knew it. The next time I think about taking a stand I'm going to take a nap instead.

TOTAL INNOCENCE
(THE VERY WORST KIND OF GUILT)

Aunt Carol drove me home from school today. You remember, Dumb Diary, that my aunt is an office lady at our school now. She is engaged to Assistant Principal Devon, who is Angeline's uncle, which has forced me to be related to Angeline somehow.

I have not lost hope, yet; being engaged to somebody is the first step toward divorcing them, so this whole situation could change for me. (I guess I just like to look on the bright side.)

Anyway, since Aunt Carol is getting married soon, everything in her life revolves around the wedding. Here's an example of a conversation a person might have with a person who has become a fiancé:

ME: Did you see on the news that there was a big flood in Wheretheheckistan?

AUNT CAROL: No, but if there's a flood here, I'll be in trouble because my dress has a five-foot-long train.

ME: Train, huh? Did I tell you my idea about Angeline's face and a train?

AUNT CAROL: No, but speaking of Angeline's face, my bouquet is going to have some flowers in it the exact color of her eyes.

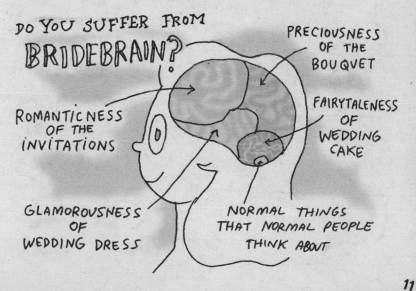

DO YOU SUFFER FROM

BRIDEBRAIN?

PRECIOUSNESS OF THE BOUQUET

FAIRYTALENESS OF WEDDING CAKE

ROMANTICNESS OF THE INVITATIONS

GLAMOROUSNESS OF WEDDING DRESS

NORMAL THINGS THAT NORMAL PEOPLE THINK ABOUT

In between her description of the **awful old-people music** they'll be playing, and the **awful old-people food** they'll be serving, Aunt Carol complained that she also has the job of making, distributing, and counting all those votes I was telling you about, so Isabella and I will probably be the first humans on Earth to know who won what.

I called Isabella and told her, and she was so excited to know we'd be first that she made a noise like Mom makes when Dad forgets to put the toilet seat down, but without all the swearing that comes afterward.

mom also made that sound once when I was little and I used her bra to play THE HUMAN FLY

Wednesday 04

Dear Dumb Diary,

Can you imagine how great school would be if you didn't have to get an education in it? Like, if all you did was just go in every day and hang around and not do anything important? It would be like being a teacher.

PLUS I COULD USE MY STUDENTS AS SERVANTS

I looked around for some accent stuff on TV tonight and I found one show where the people had French accents. The French accents made everything sound like you might like to eat it.

Like if you see the words, **"pie à la mode,"** in a restaurant that means **"pie with ice cream."** Doesn't that sound good? Here's another: **"head lice à la mode."** That means you have head lice but at least you still get to have ice cream. Doesn't that sound better than just having head lice?

ZIT

Le Pimple à la face
(BETTER, RIGHT?)

Also, it's amazing that the dogs in Paris **ACTUALLY UNDERSTAND FRENCH.** It took us three years to teach Stinker not to go wee wee on the rug. I can't imagine how hard it is to teach dogs a foreign language. Maybe I'll try to teach Stinker a couple of French words, although I probably won't start with **"oui oui."** (That's pronounced **"wee wee,"** Dumb Diary, and that's how French people say **"yes"**—which just has to make them laugh all the time.)

Like, you could be all, "Oh, officer, was my whole family in the house when the meteor hit it?"

And he'd be all, "Wee wee."

And then the two of you would just laugh and laugh.

Oh, French people, I just love how foreign you are!

french people probably ballet everywhere they go.

Thursday 05

Dear Dumb Diary,

Meat Loaf Day, of course. Thursday is always Meat Loaf Day. If you buy your lunch at school, lunchroom monitor Bruntford is there to make you eat the meat loaf, in spite of the fact that it smells like baked armpit.

Our opinion of Miss Bruntford has changed, I guess. She is still as mean and nasty as, let's say, a cow with thingies that could shoot flames at you. But when Miss Anderson* was in love with Aunt Carol's fiancé, Miss Bruntford did go out of her way to destroy Miss Anderson's hopes and dreams, so in some ways she's really, really nice.

Still, it's easier to eat the meat loaf than to get into an argument with Miss Bruntford about it, so today I tried to make it more appetizing by saying **"meat loaf"** with a French accent. But contorting my mouth in French ways just made me gag more.

*Miss Anderson is my art teacher and is pretty enough to be a waitress or even sell real estate. She used to be my B.T.F. —that's like a B.F.F., but with a teacher. Like so many of the **Best Forever Relationships,** it wasn't good and it didn't last.

Isabella was doing her best to try to make me laugh while I was eating. I told her never to do that because I once heard about this girl at another school who laughed while she was eating lunch and shot spaghetti out of her nose. The teachers were afraid it was an intestine or a vein or something, so the school nurse had to come down to the lunchroom and remove it while *the entire world of her school* watched. Of course, the combination of **nasal-noodle-poisoning** and **high-intensity embarrassment** nearly killed her.

While Isabella worked even harder to make me laugh, Angeline walked by on her way to the **super-popular** table. I could have sworn that I noticed Angeline stop for a split second next to our table, as if she was thinking about sitting down.

Angeline can sit wherever she wants, of course. Everybody knows that. When you are as pretty and popular as Angeline, there is a very short list of places you cannot sit to eat your lunch.

WHERE ANGELINE CAN'T SIT TO EAT HER LUNCH

1. MARS (FOR NOW)

2. ON TOP OF THE PRESIDENT'S LUNCH

3. THAT'S PRETTY MUCH IT

I thought she was thinking about joining us, but she must have just stopped for a second to let a wedgie self-correct or something like that. (Isabella says that super-attractive people don't get the sort of wedgies that require you to go in after them like a rescue team saving a puppy stuck in a cave. They have the ability to gracefully flex their heinies in such a way that their butt, like, spits out the underpants—which sounds horrible and magnificent at the same time.)

Angeline's favorite lunch?

Flower petals with glitter and perfume.

PROBABLY.

SPIT

After lunch, we stopped by the office to see Aunt Carol and listen to her blabber on about her wedding dress and shoes and veil and all that junk. Isabella mentioned that the wedding was coming up so fast that she would be surprised if everything was ready in time.

I think this freaked out Aunt Carol a little, because she grabbed a calendar and showed it to Isabella and told her that she had plenty of time.

Then she told Isabella again that she had plenty of time and then she told me. She told us both a couple more times and then she actually told the calendar that she had plenty of time, but it almost sounded more like she was begging the calendar instead of telling it.

Nice one, Isabella. Seriously, what were you thinking?

Friday 06

Dear Dumb Diary,

Beautiful glorious news! Today they told us that something went stinkfully wrong with the heating or ventilation system or something over at Wodehouse Middle School. Supposedly it's some kind of horrible odor, maybe even poisonous. Since they think it's going to take weeks to repair, they're busing the kids to different nearby schools, and Mackerel Middle School is one of them.

I'm **THRILLED** that foreigners are coming. I love people who aren't from here! And I'll bet they're all pretty excited that they're not from here, too. I know that if I was not from here, I'd be pretty excited.

I mean, the only problem with here is that it's where I'm from. And they're not from here, so I know I already like that about them.

They're only a few miles away, but I wonder if they'll have accents. England is only a few inches from France, and they have different accents.

ENGLAND <------> France
see?

Isabella is suspicious of the Wodehouse kids, and thinks that they will probably take our stuff. Isabella has mean older brothers, so she has grown up thinking that somebody is always going to take her stuff or throw a booger at her.

This may be why Isabella wrongfully believes that every place else is worse than here, and I rightly know that every place else is better. (Except those places with weird laws like you can't dance with a monkey or wear high heels. We both agree that those places are worse.)

Isabella and me on a CRIME SPREE

Aunt Carol came over for a while tonight to visit Mom. She discovered some weight-loss pamphlets on her desk, and she was all upset that maybe somebody was telling her that she was gaining weight and now her wedding dress won't fit right.

We all told her that it was just somebody who was all jealous of her wedding.

Isabella was over for dinner tonight, so thankfully she was on hand to cheer up Aunt Carol by telling her about her cousin who was so big they just stitched two wedding dresses together. She said she could get Aunt Carol the name of the dressmakers who did it and that they also make tents, in case Aunt Carol is thinking about going camping for her honeymoon.

Isabella always has the answers. I guess I'm pretty lucky that we're best friends. It's also lucky that when Isabella is over for dinner, Dad insists that we get pizza or something like that because it's difficult to predict how nonfamily members will medically react to Mom's cooking.

once mom's porkchops made a lady's head throw up its hair

Isabella and I tried to teach Stinker some foreign words after dinner. Stinker hates cats, so I said **"gato,"** which is the one Spanish word I know. It means **"cat."** But he didn't do anything, so Isabella thinks he might be deaf. She tried the one bit of sign language she knows, which also happens to be cat. Stinker sniffed the air, which she said proves he's deaf because he was sniffing for a cat.

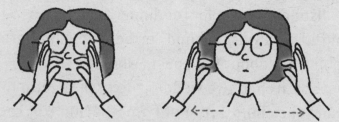

But I don't think he's deaf. Anytime your hands go near your face, Stinker thinks you have food, so he goes on alert to figure out what you have and then determines how hard he wishes for you to drop it, which is a dog's favorite way to eat things.

If I ever open a restaurant for dogs, the waitstaff will walk back and forth past the dog's table, eating whatever he had ordered. Every time, they will just drop some of it on the floor.

Oh, and the dogs' water glasses will be filled from the toilet because Stinker also seems to enjoy that, too.

Saturday 07

Dear Dumb Diary,

Angeline called **FIRST THING THIS MORNING!!!** She is one of those insane people that gets up early on days she doesn't have to get up early.

The project we're doing isn't due for weeks, but Angeline wants to **PLAN AHEAD.**

I was also **PLANNING AHEAD,** Angeline. I was **PLANNING** on putting it off until the day before it was due, which is a totally legitimate kind of planning. So you're not the only one capable of **PLANNING,** Blondwad.

Anyway, Angeline is a **PARENT WHISPERER,** one of those people that can talk to parents and understand their odd language. She told Mom all about the project, so now, of course, Mom will be on my back until it's done. She also told my mom about the plan she had for us today, and how she and her mom would be by in a while to pick me up . . .

. . . **to go take pictures of graffiti somewhere.**

Angeline's mom, you might remember, Dumb Diary, looks a lot like Angeline (you know, after Angeline is deformed into a mom) but has hair that is even worse than mine.

She and Angeline seem to have a very strange mother-daughter relationship in which they talk nicely to each other. What's that about, right?

Her mom is really nice to me because her brother, Assistant Principal Devon, is marrying my aunt Carol, which I think will make her my cousin or grandma-in-law or something like that if the divorce I'm hoping for doesn't come through (fingers crossed).

I like Angeline's mom, which makes me wonder if Angeline was adopted. Or built in some twisted doll factory.

EYELASH

HIDEOUSLY PERFECT HEADS

HAND LOTION

We drove up to the supermarket and tried to figure out something we could say about the graffiti we found, but it was mostly just people's names written on the wall out by the trash cans. (Hey, here's a tip, graffitists, if you want us to read your name so bad that you'll paint it on a wall, why don't you PRINT CLEARLY?)

Nice idea you had, Angeline. We'll have to find something better than this for our dumb project.

Sunday 08

Dear Dumb Diary,

Isabella and I talked for a long time on the phone this morning, which usually makes Dad nuts, because, as a dad, his conversations with his friends go something like this:

DAD: Hey.
DAD'S FRIEND: Hey.
DAD: Lawnmower.
DAD'S FRIEND: Lawnmower football.
DAD: Gas-tank football crescent-wrench plumbing.
DAD'S FRIEND: Bye.
DAD: Bye.

And this is a friend he hasn't talked to in four years.

But on Sundays, Dad just tries to relax and leave everybody else alone because if he starts talking about you making the most of your time, Mom will start talking about him making the most of his time right when Dad is really focused on making the least of his time by watching TV and **butt-sitting-on**. So I can talk on the phone for a **loooooooonnnnngggg** time on Sundays.

The Harmony of Mutual worthlessness

I was trying to talk Isabella into the idea of getting accents, because I think it would be cooler if we could talk to each other in accents and nobody could understand us. Then Isabella told me that she heard about this girl from another school or something who fell asleep in class with a permanent marker in her mouth and it leaked and left a blue spot on her tongue for the rest of her life. Now, the total humiliation has forever deprived her of the right to stick her tongue back out at you when you stick your tongue out at her. Who could live that way?

UNABLE TO
↑TONGUEFULLY
RESPOND

I can't always figure out what point Isabella is trying to make with these stories. I think the connection here was that this story had to do with a mouth, which is the main hole accents come out of.

But for somebody who doesn't like kids from other schools, Isabella sure knows a lot about them.

Monday 09

Dear Dumb Diary,

The visitors from **the faraway middle
school** arrived today. Okay, it's only a couple
miles away, but still. I had a close encounter with
one today and, *excellently,* so did Angeline.

Here's how it went: We were in English
class and Mr. Evans was talking about his dumb
**understanding-cultures-through-
writing thing,** and he started giving us a haiku
lesson.

A haiku is a traditional Japanese three-line
poem that has five syllables in the first line, seven
in the next line, and then five in the last line, which
is useful to know in case you ever find yourself in a
position where you're inspired to write a beautiful
poem, but you can't be bothered to spend any more
than seventeen syllables on the project.

So, Mr. Evans read us a few, and I guess
they're kind of pretty. Most of them seemed to be
about flowers and birds. Then he asked us to write
one, but he only gave us a couple minutes. I really

don't think it was fair to make us read them out loud, but he did.

Anyway, this was mine:

Five syllables here.
And now you got seven more.
And now five. Happy?

When Evans is angry he pumps extra blood through his face so that his big ugly head-vein throbs at you. He gave me a couple of throbs and then called on Angeline. This, unfortunately, was her haiku:

The sparrow's music
Is brighter and lovelier
Than festive feathers.

It got a little round of applause, of course, because even Angeline's intestinal gas would get a little round of applause.

But before they could all erect a big gold statue to the memory of how excellent Angeline's haiku was, a girl in the back—one I had not noticed when I came in—raised her hand. She was one of the new Wodehouse Middle School kids. And Mr. Evans called on her: **"Yes, *Colette*."**

That's right Dumb Diary; *"Colette."* That's a French name, which means it sounds 25% more attractive than a non-French name—like if her name was Barney.

And get this: She is *prettier* than Angeline. **A LOT PRETTIER!** And she's doing it without the unfair advantage of blond hair. In fact, *Colette's* hair is black. It's as black and silky and shiny as if you crossed a puppy with a unicorn. And gave it black hair.

Okay, that particular animal didn't come out as attractive as I thought it might. Anyway, *Colette* has really pretty French-looking hair. This was her haiku:

Hey bird. Thanks loads but
Your song won't make up for the
Bird poo on our car.

Colette's haiku got applause *and a laugh.* I think she really was aiming it directly at Angeline, because right on the last line, I saw her look straight at Angeline and smile, but not a nice smile. It was more like the kind of smile a beautiful fairy lumberjack might make just before it took a chain saw to an annoying blond tree.

And, with that, it was as though Angeline's haiku was wiped off the face of the Earth, as easily as you might wipe her face off a train.

Right after class, we caught up to *Colette* in the hall, her dizzying beauty causing boys to blow along after her like sad little leaves caught up in a hurricane of **Pure Girlness**.

"Nice haiku, *Colette*," Isabella said.

And I adorably added, "I wish that haiku had been my-ku."

And Isabella had to add, "You should, Jamie. It was way better than yours."

Which was really uncalled for. I let Isabella know that by thinking up a really great comeback about two hours later, which I forgot by the time I saw her again.

Shut up. It was a really *really* great comeback!

Tuesday 10

Dear Dumb Diary,

    Colette sat with us at lunch today. The name *Colette* is French, so I guess I wasn't surprised to see her eating **FRENCH** fries. I asked her if she had French toast for breakfast and then almost immediately regretted it because she looked at me like I look at my little cousin when I see him putting something in his nose.

Fortunately, Isabella was there and she is really good at conversation.

"So, what is it that you're after?" Isabella asked, in what might not have been her best conversational effort to date.

"After?" *Colette* said with innocent cuteness. I had to explain how Isabella is just naturally suspicious of everybody because of her mean older brothers. *Colette* just smiled really big and said, ***"Oh, I know something about getting even with mean older brothers."***

SUSPICIOUS EYES

HANDS THAT WOULD BE HAPPIER AS FISTS

MOUTH THAT HAS BITTEN MORE PEOPLE THAN AN AVERAGE MOUTH

I am not a little sister, so I don't speak the language these two were talking, but I managed to pick up bits and pieces of what *Colette* was telling Isabella, like:

"Loop the rope once only. Any more than that, and you could send them to the emergency room."

"Use spoiled cat food. It's the worst, and don't get any on your hands. It could blind you."

And . . .

"Make sure they understand that if they tell the police, it will be way worse next time."

Isabella took notes that looked better than any she had ever taken before, and when *Colette* left, she said, "That may be the finest little sister that has ever lived. This is a level of treachery and payback that I never even imagined."

Isabella looked a little like Aunt Carol did the day she told me she was engaged.

Wednesday 11

Dear Dumb Diary,

Isabella got a speck of glitter in her eye during art class today and had to go down to the office to see the school nurse. I had a very hard time believing that she needed medical attention, because I have seen Isabella endure things that would make professional spies tell you where the secret plans were hidden.

The nurse couldn't see the glitter speck at all. Isabella said that maybe her tear hole ate it, but the nurse said that couldn't happen. I'm not so sure. Almost nothing has come out of Isabella's tear holes since I've known her.

After English, I met up with Isabella outside the nurse's office, and we stopped by the main office to talk to Aunt Carol.

Isabella asked about the ballots. She wanted to know if they'd been written yet and if they were ready to be handed out yet and had she heard about how wedding cakes were totally out of fashion now and most celebrities were having wedding pies instead.

Aunt Carol had not done anything about the voting stuff yet, and Isabella was the second girl to ask her today and she wanted to know exactly where Isabella heard that wedding cakes were no longer "in."

Isabella couldn't remember, but she thinks it was on the news or in the papers or online. Maybe all three.

I thought it was pretty helpful, but Aunt Carol acted all mad like it was Isabella's fault that the fashion world had lost interest in cake. Not exactly a news flash. One look at those fashion models, and I could have told you that they had tragically lost interest in cake a long time ago.

OTHER THINGS FASHION MODELS HAVE LOST INTEREST IN

COMFORTABLE SHOES

sweats

WALKING NORMAL

Thursday 12

Dear Dumb Diary,

Turns out that we also got a lunch lady from Wodehouse Middle School. Today, she made the best school lunch that has ever been served in Mackerel Middle School.

It was called beef **pâté**. That's pronounced **pa-TAY**, which might be French for meat loaf, if Isabella is right. Truthfully, it didn't taste much better than the turd loaf that they usually serve us on Thursdays, but you could tell it was **A LOT BETTER** because there was a little sprig of parsley on the plate, which makes everything more appealing.

CRAZY KILLER CLOWN HIDING UNDER YOUR BED

WITH PARSLEY SPRIG

Now that I think about it, your foreign-ness is sort of *the sprig of parsley* sitting next to you on the plate.

We might never have known the pâté's origins, except that *Colette* sat with us today at lunch and her sharp sense of taste identified it as a Wodehouse recipe.

I had a lot of questions for her about her middle school, like how it was different and if they had accents there or any troublesome blond infestations like the one we have.

She wisely knew immediately who I was talking about (I pointed a little), and said that there were some girls at her school who also bleached their hair and wore too much makeup. (Isabella and I looked at each other, because we both know that Angeline doesn't do either one, but it's rude to contradict someone when they are lying in a way that you enjoy.)

Colette also said they did things at her school like voting for BEST FRIENDS, MOST BEAUTIFUL, MOST ARTISTIC, and stuff like that, but the whole ventilation problem probably canceled it this year, so now she wouldn't get to do it.

Isabella told her not to worry. She said that the voting at Mackerel Middle School would include the kids that are here temporarily from Wodehouse. I have no idea how Isabella knows that, but she is a total expert ON EVERYTHING, which is why she wins MOST CLEVER every year.

PROOF OF HER CLEVERNESS

INVENTED THE REMOTE CONTROL LABRADOR WHEN SHE WAS FOUR.

DEVELOPED A NEW WEIGHT-LOSS TECHNIQUE WHEN SHE WAS FIVE

DISCOVERED THE FOOTPRINT OF A VERY SMALL BIGFOOT AT THE BEACH LAST JUNE.

FRIDAY 13

Dear Dumb Diary,

Isabella is sleeping over tonight. We went through our regular list of sleepover activities quicker than usual. I'm telling you, if there was such a thing as a **Professional Prank Caller**, Isabella would be able to choose that career over the other two she usually says she wants to do: **Master Catcher of Master Criminals** or if that doesn't work out, a **Master Criminal**. Also, she likes Dental Hygienist.

Note to Parents: if you are reading this, we **didn't** make prank calls. if you are me, Jamie, reading this later, we **totally DID.**

After making a few international prank calls, Isabella started asking me about Aunt Carol and the voting and said we should just tell her that we'll take care of everything, since she's busy with a failing wedding. I really did **NOT** want to take on this huge extra project, since I have been very busy avoiding the huge project I already have to do with Angeline.

Isabella is very persuasive, and I finally agreed to talk to Aunt Carol, but only if Isabella went along with me on the accent project. She said okay and started teaching me to mispronounce words like her grandma does.

Isabella's grandma has an accent, but it always sounds a little gross to me. (Sorry, Isabella, I love your grandma, but she looks like a jack-o'-lantern that was run over by a bus.)

But when Isabella speaks like her grandma, I guess it sounds cool. It doesn't make her sound smart or sophisticated exactly, but it does make her sound like she's from someplace else.

When we tried the accent on Stinker, he did not understand us, even when we screamed in order to tolerantly accept his deafness. I'm really good at this accent, but I'm not sure I have the confidence to try it in public. (Oh, by the way, I think it's an Italian accent, which totally works for me because I love Italian stuff like SpaghettiOs and that chocolate-vanilla-strawberry ice cream, except the strawberry part.)

WANTED

But Isabella says that if Italy ever catches the guy that invented CANNED SPAGHETTI, HE WILL BE JAILED FOR CRIMES AGAINST PASTA.

I called Aunt Carol and she sounded kind of like maybe she might want us to help with the voting. She's been very busy trying to track down information on wedding pies, and that has taken a lot of time. Isabella had me tell her that while she's at it, she should look into **bridal clogs,** which are the new shoe that all the trendy young brides in Hollywood are wearing. They're made out of wood and are supercool. And bridesmaids' dresses now are supposed to be brown and poofy.

I had never heard of either of these fads, but Isabella knows an awful lot.

HOW CUTE WOULD IT BE TO MAKE BEAVERS EAT YOUR SHOES OUT OF A TREE?

Saturday 14

Dear Dumb Diary,

Angeline called **FIRST THING THIS MORNING.** She woke up early **AGAIN** on a day she doesn't have to go to school. Although, as it turns out, today we *did* go to school.

Since Angeline is totally comfortable talking to parents, she also told my mom about the plan she had for us today.

(I really can't stand when people talk to my parents like they're people.)

She got permission from Assistant Principal Devon—her uncle Dan—to go in on a Saturday . . .

. . . **and take pictures in** THE BOYS' BATHROOM!!!

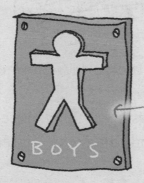

DON'T LET THE LITTLE GINGERBREAD MAN ON THE SIGN FOOL YOU. IT DOES NOT SMELL LIKE A BAKERY IN THERE

That's right. As if regular **PUBLIC** graffiti wasn't stupid enough, today she wanted to understand the culture of boys by taking pictures of the things they write on their stinky walls.

I was going to totally refuse, based on the **WEAPONS–GRADE GROSSNESS** of boys' toilets, but Isabella overheard everything and insisted on going with us.

← ME HAUNTED BY GHOSTS OF BOY TOILETS

And we went, Dumb Diary. We went where the boys went.

But right now my ears are ringing like crazy and I need some aspirin and some rest. I'll tell you about it tomorrow.

Sunday 15

Dear Dumb Diary,

It's early Sunday morning, and my ears are almost done ringing. Let me tell you about yesterday.

My mom dropped us off and waited outside the school. We checked in at the office and went down to one of the boys' ucky bathrooms.

I was really not interested at all in this little mission because of a nightmare I have from time to time.

In it, I have to use the bathroom really bad, but I can't find a girls' bathroom, and finally have to use the boys' bathroom. When I open the door and go in, there's Hudson Rivers, the eighth-cutest boy in my grade, who doesn't even seem that surprised to see me, which is odd, because I am pretty sure we are destined to be together one day (I think he knows it, too). But when I see myself in the mirror I am an orangutan and that seems to me like something a dude would notice about his future wife.

So I was opening the door very quietly and whispering "Hello? Hello?" and checking my feet to make sure they were not sprouting thumbs, which Isabella felt was taking too long, so she helpfully shoved me in.

Writing graffiti will get you in a TON of trouble at our school, and they clean it off as quickly as they can, but they don't do it every day so Angeline figured we might be able to find some for our report.

We took turns taking lots of pictures with Angeline's camera, and that made it seem less like poking around in a horrifying bathroom and more like we were *Attractive Crime Scene Investigators* looking for some murder clues amid short poems about doody and the very peculiar wall fixtures that sort of look like pretty little fountains with giant mints in them. Trust me: They aren't.

STYLIN'

It wasn't until we started reading the graffiti that I started to get mad.

Look, many boys can be excellent artists and writers. But they're just not doing their best work in bathrooms *on general subjects.* And *that's* what made me mad.

Well, that's not exactly what made me mad.

YOUR BASIC DUMB
TYPICAL BOY GRAFFITI

What made me mad was what they wrote about Angeline. Because even though their work on general topics was poor (topics like stinkiness and doo-doo, and whether or not a certain teacher has artificial parts), on the subject of Angeline, this probably **WAS** their best work. **In their lives!** I mean it was better than what they write in their book reports, better than what they draw in art class! Here's a few things I jotted down:

Angeline
I love you more than
life itself and maybe
even video games

Love

Middle School is
the east and Angeline
is the sun.

THE ANGELINE GRAFFITI

I was trying not to look angry at the flattery, and Angeline was trying not to look embarrassed by it, when Isabella screamed.

I may have touched on this before, but Isabella has awful older brothers. This means that over the years, Isabella has developed a scream that her parents can hear from miles away to let them know that her brothers are inflicting some sort of horrible torture on her. (It often involves spit.)

Inside a tiny bathroom, when we were all standing **aboutthisclosetogether**, Isabella's **brother-scream** was crippling. Angeline and I nearly fainted.

And here's why Isabella screamed: In one of the stalls, written in clear, bold green marker, it said:

VOTE JAMIE KELLY FOR PRETTIEST

I didn't know what to say. But Isabella did, and she said it: "I guess maybe not everybody thinks you're the prettiest girl in the world, huh, Angeline?"

Which was true, I guess. But she said it over and over to Angeline all the way back to her house when we dropped her off. And she even yelled it out the window as we drove away.

It never really seemed to bother Angeline that much, but it did seem to bother my mom quite a bit. She asked Angeline to get her copies of all the photos we took to see what else had been written on the subject of her daughter on the bathroom wall. Apparently, this is just something moms are curious about.

I HEARD ABOUT THIS MOM WHO STUCK HER NOSE SO FAR IN HER DAUGHTER'S BUSINESS THAT THEY HAD TO GO TO THE HOSPITAL TO GET IT REMOVED.

Monday 16

Dear Dumb Diary,

It's strange, but the graffiti in the boys' bathroom made me feel so confident about myself that I decided to try out my new accent just a little bit today around my locker. I was disappointed at how intolerant the kids at my school are of people who sound like they might be from other countries.

At first they smiled, and then they laughed, and then when I didn't laugh, they asked what was wrong with me.

But Mr. VanDoy walked by and nicely asked me if I was choking on something, which is a pretty good indicator that I was really doing a very good accent.

SICKENING SOUNDS ARE CRITICAL TO MANY FOREIGN ACCENTS

Angeline ran up to me in the hall and was all excited about photographing graffiti in some of **the girls' bathrooms** now and I told her to go ahead and do it by herself, and she said we had to do it together. I'm *so* sure. What does she think? That we're some sort of conjoined twins connected at the assignment?

I've actually had this nightmare

But she wouldn't drop it, so just to shut her up, I went with her into the girls' bathroom right down the hall from my locker.

There was practically no graffiti, which is really good news because I think it means we are going to fail this assignment and it will be Angeline's fault.

We photographed: 1) A small drawing of a bald guy peeking over a wall that had been mostly scrubbed off.

2) A picture of Miss Bruntford that was drawn by Isabella a month ago — and which Isabella had pointed out to me already.

3) And, unbelievably, *ANOTHER* "VOTE JAMIE KELLY FOR PRETTIEST." It looked exactly like the one we saw in the *boys'* bathroom.

It seemed obvious to me that the accent was working, even though I had only started this morning. Some girl must have been overwhelmed by it and ran in here to write this loving tribute.

When I told Isabella about the graffiti later, she said, **"Maybe you're getting prettier and we just can't tell."** I thanked her at the time, but now as I write this, it doesn't sound that nice.

I have to admit that since the graffiti is so complimentary toward me, I'm starting to warm up to Angeline's super-dumb idea.

"Maybe we should check out one of the teachers' bathrooms," I said. Isabella's head spun around like Stinker's when he hears a Cheeto hit the ground.

"I'll do it!" Isabella said. **"Let's go!"**

see? twins.

But here's the thing. You can't just barge into the teachers' bathroom and start snapping pictures. Trust me, you don't want to: Adults need **A LOT** of assorted ointments and lotions just to keep from turning into piles of dust, and you **DO NOT** want to accidentally get a look at them applying these. (It's a long story, but let's just say — Grandma. Lotion. Rash. Bare naked. Moral of story: **KNOCK FIRST.**)

Ssssssssss

eyeballs fried out by vision of grandma nudeness

Plus, I knew we needed to ask permission, but that wasn't going to be a problem, of course. I knew Aunt Carol would say yes, so all Isabella and I had to do was go to the office after lunch and ask.

Aunt Carol said *no*. Can you believe it? I'm her own niece! I was really angry and Isabella was so mad that she walked right out of the office . . .

. . . and walked right back with Angeline, who asked the exact same thing, and then Aunt Carol said okay.

WHAT?! ANGELINE! I was really mad that *another thing* came so easy to Angeline. Isabella told me not to get my panties in a wad about it, and said she knew Aunt Carol would say yes to Angeline, because generally people are nicer to other people than they are to their own relatives.

I guess I had never noticed this before, but since Isabella comes from a big family, she was born with a lot more people to be not nice to than I was. That thought calmed me down a little. Plus, I was giggling about the wadded panties.

Aunt Carol said that we wouldn't find any graffiti in the teachers' bathroom anyway, since teachers have better things to do than write on walls all day — except I couldn't help but think that's exactly what they do.

SEE?

The teachers' bathroom was pretty much like a regular person's bathroom, except for the big can of air freshener on the toilet tank, which means that they have totally given up on trying to make people think that they aren't stinking it up in there. As you get older, I think you give up on impressing others a little every year.

Like my dad has given up enough to go outside in his pajamas to get the newspaper, but he's not as old as my grandpa, who has given up enough to mow the lawn butt-naked if Grandma doesn't stop him.

I KNOW DAD HAS GIVEN UP. HE WENT OUT AND GOT THE PAPER ONCE IN MOM'S ROBE

Anyway, we couldn't find any real graffiti, except that Isabella found a little tiny heart with an arrow through it that said **D. D. +V. A.** This didn't really mean anything to me, but Isabella says the **D. D.** is for sure **Dan Devon** (Assistant Principal Devon), and the **V. A.** could be **Valerie Anderson,** my art teacher who is pretty enough to be a waitress. She's the one who tried to steal Assistant Principal Devon from my aunt Carol.

I figured it would be best to just wipe it off and not even tell Aunt Carol about it, and Isabella agreed. So she went out and asked Aunt Carol for some cleaner and a rag and then told her exactly what it was for, including the arrow through the heart—which makes it a much bigger deal than if it was just a heart alone.

D.D.
x
V. A

← LOOK
HOW
HORRIBLE

Later on, we saw Aunt Carol and Assistant Principal Devon YELL-WHISPERING at each other. You know that kind of whispering you do when you want to yell but you also want to try to keep it private? It sounds like little dogs with sore throats fighting inside a bag.

The only way adults argue louder than whispering is when they do it silently

As smart as Isabella is, I'm really surprised at her sometimes. How could she have missed how this would make Aunt Carol react?

Tuesday 17

Dear Dumb Diary,

Boy, oh boy. More culture stuff today. Mr. Evans talked about little *phrases of wisdom* like, **THE GRASS IS ALWAYS GREENER ON THE OTHER SIDE OF THE FENCE.** He said these can illustrate the values of a culture. He asked what we thought the **Grass-Is-Greener** one meant, and I said it means that your dad is about as good at lawn care as mine.

This only got me one throb of the forehead-vein. Maybe a throb and a half, so I was probably pretty close to the right answer.

THROB DECATHROB ARMED THROBBERY

Just like he did with the haiku, Mr. Evans asked us to write down our favorite phrase in class. Also like the haiku, he made us read them out loud.

Here's a sample of what we said:

Angeline: **YOU CAN'T JUDGE A BOOK BY ITS COVER.**

Me: **A BIRD IN THE HAND IS WORTH TWO IN THE BUSH.**

Isabella: **WHOEVER SMELT IT, DEALT IT.**

But Mr. Evans said that really wasn't a *phrase of wisdom* exactly, so Isabella quickly offered:

WHOEVER DENIED IT, SUPPLIED IT.

Evans said, **"WRONG AGAIN,"** and Isabella tossed out:

WHOEVER LOOKS THE MOST AT EASE IS THE ONE WHO CUT THE CHEESE.

And:

WHOEVER SMILES OR LAUGHS OUT LOUD IS THE ONE THAT MADE THE CLOUD.

I know for a fact that Isabella has a lot of wisdom on this theme, but Mr. Evans didn't give her a chance to share it all. He just throbbed and asked *Colette* for hers.

Colette stood up to read her phrase of wisdom, swinging her hair around like some glorious, inky-black vampire cape. "I don't really have one, Mr. Evans, but I wanted to say you're all really lucky to go to this school, and thanks for helping us out while they fix our ventilation system." And she flashed this grin that made Angeline's famous smile look like a banana peel hurriedly stuck on a dirty snowman for a mouth.

Mr. Evans didn't know what to say. I think he was temporarily charmed. I think the whole class was. She was *good*. And it was during that pause that Angeline did something **REALLY** weird.

She stood up and said that she wanted to give Mr. Evans a *status report* on how our graffiti project was going, and before Evans could even say **okay,** she showed the whole class the graffiti pictures including the ones that said VOTE JAMIE KELLY FOR PRETTIEST.

I got some applause and an **OH YEAH, DAT'S RIGHT!** (thanks, Isabella) and I blushed. Angeline just smiled and put the pictures back in her folder.

See how confident she is that she can't lose? She'll even tell people to vote for me, knowing full well that they'll vote for *her.* How mean can you get?

When somebody you don't like does something NICE FoR you it's like if YouR DOG FarTed Your favorite Song.

Wednesday 18

Dear Dumb Diary,

   Aunt Carol stopped by after school today and **FINALLY** asked me to take care of the voting stuff.
   She seemed a little twitchy, and later Mom told me that planning a wedding is complicated, and it's making Aunt Carol a little flustered.
   When Mom left the room, Dad summed it up by saying that the wedding is driving Aunt Carol insane and that soon Mom will be driven insane and everyone on Earth will also be insane if they don't just hurry up and get this over with.
   I doubt that Dad will be writing greeting cards anytime soon.

DAD CARDS

Even though it was late, I called Isabella to tell her that Aunt Carol had finally offered up the voting and she went, "YES," the same way Dad does when some guy on one of his sports shows sinks a goal or pulls a groin or touches a down or whatever.

I used my accent a little at school today, and I also tried it on Mom and Dad tonight. Mom just said it wasn't nice to talk like that. Dad laughed at first, and then Mom shot him this dirty look and he repeated what Mom said.

Mom's wrong, but I think Dad has just learned, like Stinker did, that sometimes it's much easier on your neck not to pull on the leash.

Oh, one more thing. I noticed *Colette* prettily sharpening her pencil today. Actually, a few of us noticed her doing it.

Do pretty girls take special classes where they learn to do everything prettily? Or is *Colette* just naturally more appetizing because her name is French?

A teacher at PRETTY SCHOOL teaching GLAMOROUS PIT ITCHERY.

And speaking of Stinker, it seems like he is beginning to understand my accent. This makes me think that he is very, very smart, or, even likelier, has a brain problem. I forget the formula for determining how old a dog is exactly, but in dog years, I'm pretty sure that Stinker is dead already.

IS STINKER DEAD? CHECK THE EVIDENCE

WON'T DO WHAT HE'S TOLD

DECAYING ODOR

NOT PLEASANT TO LOOK AT

LIKE MOST DEAD THINGS, DOESN'T UNDERSTAND SPANISH

Thursday 19

Dear Dumb Diary,

    Isabella looked awful today. She was up most of the night getting the voting categories together, and she came in an hour and a half early to use the copier in the office to make enough ballots for everyone. I thought this was something we were going to do together—but Isabella said she found out that the Wodehouse kids are going back next week and she wanted them to be included in the voting. Isabella is *so* considerate.

DON'T TRY THIS AT HOME. I KNEW SHE WAS TOO TIRED TO PUNCH ME.

Here's what the rules are:

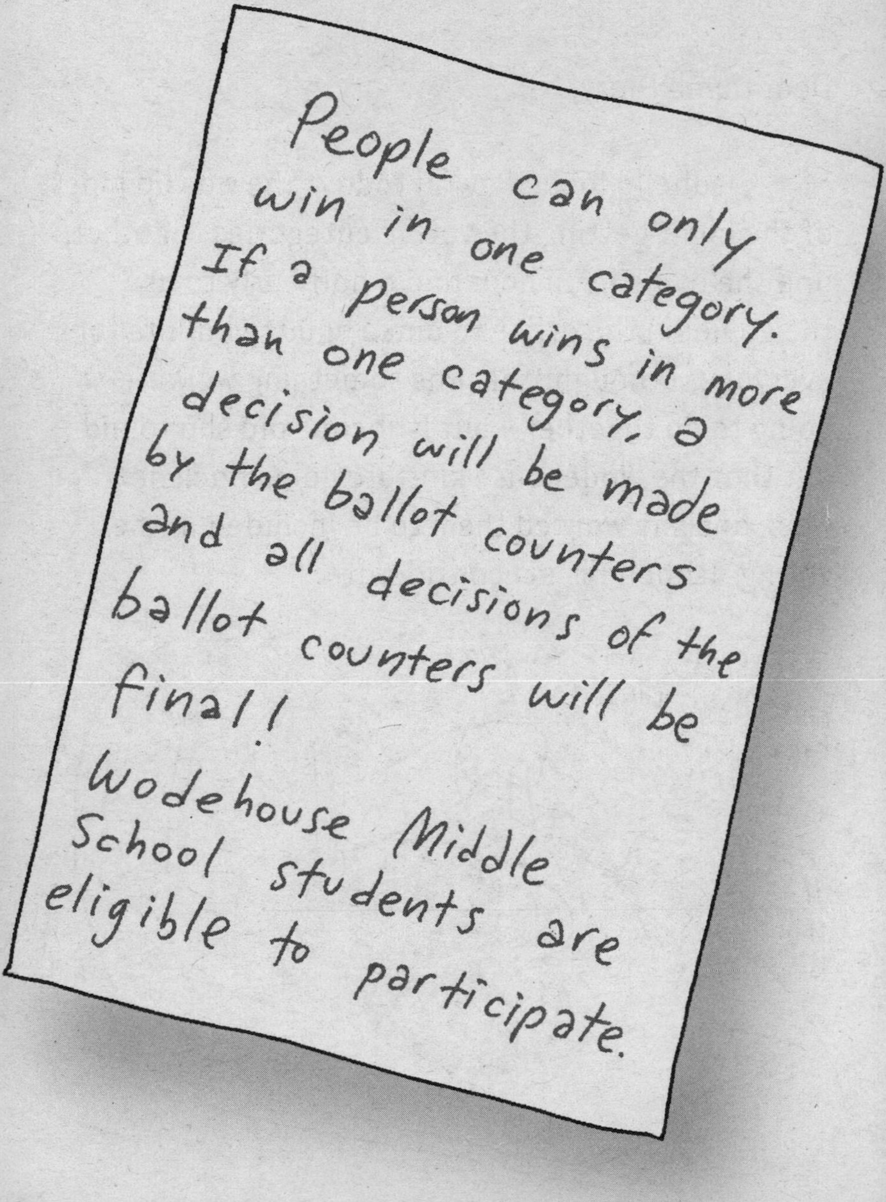

People can only win in one category. If a person wins in more than one category, a decision will be made by the ballot counters and all decisions of the ballot counters will be final!!

Wodehouse Middle School students are eligible to participate.

And here are the categories Isabella came up with:

Most Artistic
Most Clever
Prettiest Girl
Cutest Boy
Funniest
Best Friends

She wanted to have **DISGUSTINGEST, STINKIEST,** and **DUMBEST,** but she says she knows that the school would never allow those categories, and they would take the voting project away from her. I can't imagine how hard it was for Isabella not to put those mean categories on there. It shows how nice she really is.

if people knew how hard it is FOR MEAN PEOPLE to TRY NOT TO BE MEAN, they WOULD CONSIDER them NICER than NICE PEOPLE

They announced the voting and where to get the ballots, and that they had to be turned in to the office by Friday afternoon. Isabella and I will count them, put the results together, and announce the winners next Friday.

IN ADDITION TO VOTING, ISABELLA AND I SHOULD BE IN CHARGE OF THE ENTIRE GOVERNMENT

OUR CHANGES:

We'll replace the American Eagle with a duck which is a nicer and funnier BIRD

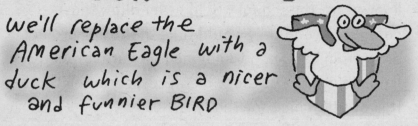

OLD mean Gross Guys won't be in charge of everything

Actually, we'll replace the Eagle with a koala which is even cuter. And the old GROSS GUYS are going to be koalas, too.

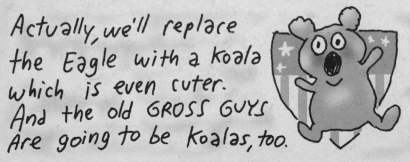

Friday 20

Dear Dumb Diary,

All day, people asked us to call them early and tell them what the results were before anybody else found out. I had no idea there was so much pressure on the government, which is kind of what we are now that we are in charge of voting. I told Isabella that stress like this is probably what turned Washington's hair white, but she said that was just a wig he wore.

Can you believe that? Plus, of all the wig colors he could have chosen, he went with the **platinum blond**. For sure, now Lincoln—a **brunette** and proud of it—is my favorite president.

probably all stuck-up and trying to steal Lincoln's girlfriend all the time

Angeline stopped by my house this afternoon and dropped off the boys' bathroom pictures that my mom had asked to see. She wasn't even polite enough to stick her nose into our business about the voting. It's because she's so confident that she's going to win, which is a pretty rude thing to know.

when people are too RUDE to BUTT IN, it deprives polite people of their right to tell them to BUTT OUT

Isabella is sleeping over tonight, but she had no interest in crank calls or accent practice. All she wanted to do was count votes. She went over them a few times and wouldn't let me see. Then she said she wanted to go over all of them again tomorrow because there were a couple of things she didn't quite understand.

except for awesome PJs, Isabella was as boring as an adult

Saturday 21

Dear Dumb Diary,

Angeline didn't call this morning, which would have been nice, except it was her that didn't do it. And I woke up early anyway. She got me all used to her calls and then stopped calling. Leave it to Angeline to wake you up without actually doing it.

Mom looked at the pictures we took and didn't have any complaints. I'll give them back to Angeline on Monday.

Isabella was making little diagrams and puzzling over the ballots most of the day. She took time out for only a couple of crank calls, but really I don't think her heart was in them.

IS YOUR Refrigerator running?

YES...

THAT'S GOOD Because your food could Spoil if it wasn't

ISABELLA'S WORST CRANK CALL EVER

Isabella was still refusing to share the voting results with me by the afternoon, and when I pointed out that the project was supposed to go to Aunt Carol who is **MY AUNT,** she said that we never would have gotten our hands on them if it hadn't been for the things Isabella had done.

And then Isabella admitted what she had done. I'm telling you, it seems like Isabella is **ALWAYS** admitting something. Although it's beginning to sound more like bragging and less like a confession every time.

Turns out that Isabella has been freaking out Aunt Carol about the wedding since she found out that she had been given the responsibility for the voting. Isabella got her all frazzled about the schedule for the wedding and her weight. She made up the stuff about wedding pies and bridal clogs. And she was the one that faked the little heart graffiti in the teachers' bathroom.

Isabella says that it's super easy to freak out adults when they're planning something as big as a wedding. And she said she knew it would only take a little bit of extra stress to make Aunt Carol turn over the voting project to us.

"And you'll notice that I was right, and that's why I always win **Most Clever**," she said, and then smiled that smile that always comes with a big crack of thunder in movies.

Still, it was kind of mean to manipulate Aunt Carol that way. But I suppose no real harm was done.

Isabella helped me practice her grandma's exotic accent, probably because she felt guilty about her little plan. Well, maybe not *guilty.* I'm not sure Isabella ever feels guilty.

There should be a word for the kind of guilt people like Isabella feel: It's guilt, but nowhere near as heavy. Maybe she gets **Diet-Guilt.**

Other QUALITY PRODUCTS AVAILABLE AT ISABELLAMART

Sunday 22

Dear Dumb Diary,

    Isabella slept over again last night. I didn't exactly invite her, but she really wanted to stay, so we made a weekend out of it.

    She was already up and staring out the window when I woke up this morning. She was holding one of the pictures we took in the boys' bathroom.

    "Notice anything?" she asked.

    I noticed that it was a pretty good picture of Isabella making a pretty dumb face.

    "Anything else?" she asked.

Nothing. In the background, you could see Angeline, who had her back turned, which gave you a good look at the back of her head and the back of her butt.

Isabella put the picture away and showed me the ballots.

Angeline got **100** votes for **PRETTIEST**. *Colette* got **90**. *I got 15*. MAN! Can you believe that??

"If it hadn't been for Angeline's campaigning . . . if it hadn't been for the graffiti," Isabella said. "If it hadn't been for Angeline showing the pictures of the graffiti around, you wouldn't have picked up those fifteen votes, and *Colette* would have won."

Then, Isabella packed up her stuff, took the ballots, and went home.

Dear Dumb Diary,

Aunt Carol drove me to school today and was in a much better mood than she had been last week. She said she had a **Big Super-Fun Surprise,** but wasn't ready to share it just yet.

You always have to be a little suspicious of things adults say are fun. If they designed amusement parks just for adults, they would look like this:

Angeline sat with us at lunch today, and incredibly, so did *Colette.* This made some of the other popular kids sit at our table, which Isabella hardly even noticed, even though our regular table had taken on a much snazzier look. You could almost taste the cuteness in the air.

I used my new accent a little, and some of the kids I don't know very well tried to ignore it. **They thought it was totally for real!** How funny is that?

BLONDWAD AMAZED BY MY EXCELLENT ACCENT I BET

AMAZED BY MY ACCENT

Isabella started talking about how much she could use a little vacation, and how she wished there was a way to close the school for a few weeks.

And *Colette* said, "That's actually pretty easy to do."

Isabella looked *Colette* right in the eyes and then just stood up and walked out of the lunchroom and hardly talked the rest of the day.

We even saw PINSETTI HANG A PLUMBER'S SMILE AND Isabella didn't say a WORD

Tuesday 24

Dear Dumb Diary,

Colette wasn't in English today. In fact, none of the Wodehouse Middle-schoolers were in school today. It turns out that they're gone; all plucked from our loving grasps like little flowers whose ventilation systems don't stink anymore.

It's at times like this that we have to ask ourselves, **WHO IS THE REAL VICTIM HERE?** And then right away we must answer ourselves, **JAMIE IS THE REAL VICTIM.** If ourselves answer any other way, then we need to tell ourselves to just shut up.

Colette, with her gentle ability to make Angeline less beautiful, combined with some skills that actually seemed to frighten Isabella a little, was a really good friend for us to own. Now she's gone, and it just doesn't seem fair that there is somebody that pretty that Angeline is not forced to look at every single day.

Wednesday 25

Dear Dumb Diary,

I miss *Colette* already. She was well on her way to being the most popular girl in our school. They must love her over at Wodehouse Middle School. I wonder if she would transfer permanently to Mackerel if we offered her some bonuses.

Thursday 26

Dear Dumb Diary,

Aunt Carol called my house first thing today to see if I could do a favor for her at lunch. As it turns out, she also wanted Isabella and Angeline to help because, she said, she wants us all to be close friends. **Yuck, right?**

Aunt Carol had to drive some student files over to Wodehouse Middle School today, and she wanted me to run in and deliver the files because she's been having some difficulty walking . . .

. . . because of her bridal clogs!

That's right. She found some wooden clogs somewhere and has been wearing them to try to get her feet accustomed to them before the wedding. I really should have said something.

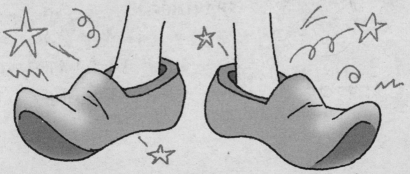

Aunt Carol parked the car and the three of us took the folders inside. Wodehouse Middle School looked exactly like Mackerel Middle School, but it smelled different. It was hard to identify. Was it school beef pâté? Boys'-bathroom-smell? Band-aid found at the bottom of a public pool?

I figured that it was a lingering odor from whatever they had to fix in the ventilation system.

ALL SCHOOL FRAGRANCES ARE A COMBINATION OF THE FIVE MAIN SMELLS

FOOT AROMA

PENCIL SHAVINGS

TEACHER ODOR

CHILD ODOR

FOOT WRAPPED IN BALONEY

We'd only gotten two steps through the door when Isabella turned to Angeline and said, "I know about the graffiti."

Angeline made a face like she had prettily swallowed a human fart.

"*You* wrote the **VOTE FOR JAMIE** stuff. We saw the marker in your back pocket in the pictures."

GULP

probably took a class in PRETTY CHOKING

"That's right," I said, having no idea what Isabella was right about. And then Angeline said things I never thought I would ever hear escape from her perfectly perfect mouth.

"Okay, I did," Angeline said quietly. "But I've washed it all off already. It was clear to me that *Colette* would have beaten me any other way. I mean, *she's gorgeous*. But even so, I knew that I *could* get enough votes for Jamie to split the vote.

"And of course she'd take the votes from *Colette,* and not from me because people don't really know *Colette.* Her position as "prettiest" is less stable than mine, because I win it every year. Sometimes I believe people don't even really think it through. They probably just automatically vote for me because they're used to voting for me."

REGULAR BRAIN

ANGELINE'S BRAIN WHICH IS NOT ONLY SMART BUT IS PROBABLY CUTELY SHAPED LIKE A NAPPING KITTEN.

"You know, it's not like **PRETTIEST** is an accomplishment," Angeline said. "It's just how you look. Being pretty is the same as being ugly. It's just something you can't really help.

"Jamie always wins **MOST ARTISTIC** and you win **MOST CLEVER.** Those are *real* things. **PRETTIEST** is so lame, but nobody ever considers me for anything else. I just wasn't about to let my one lame category go."

Angeline had done this to make sure I took away votes from *Colette*, because she knew I wouldn't take any from her!! **Amazing!**

Angeline is as pretty and SMART AS if you crossed a UNICORN with a NERD.

okay this didn't come out like I thought it would But still

"**WHOA!** Isabella. Maybe Angeline should have won most clever," I said, and Isabella just shook her head sadly.

"No. Angeline doesn't deserve it, either. Let's find the cafeteria," she said.

The cafeteria was not hard to find. Lunchrooms have a very distinctive sound. It's the sound of chairs sliding and vegetables being thrown away.

When we got there, we asked the first kid we saw where *Colette* was, figuring, like with Angeline, everybody would know where she was.

"Colette?" he asked. "Do you mean Collie? She's over there, by herself."

even in this faraway land, their clothes are much like normal people's

And there she was, just as he said, **by herself.** Her black hair had lost its sheen, her posture was a little timid, she was picking at the meat loaf, and seemed shocked to see us.

"What happened to you?" I asked as we sat down next to her. "Did you know they're calling you 'Collie,' like a dog?"

How we found her...

SAD Little NON-CHOCOLATE MILK

HAIR HAD SADLY LOST ITS WILL TO SHIMMER

SAD LITTLE BAG OF SAD LITTLE CARROTS

SAD LITTLE SANDWICH ON NON-WHITE BREAD WITH CRUSTS

WHERE DESSERT SHOULD HAVE BEEN

But Isabella had other things on her mind. "Cat food?" Isabella said to *Colette,* who dropped her droopy head even more droopily.

"You figured it out," she said.

"Not at first," Isabella said, and then explained. "It took a while to put it together. At first, I just thought that *Colette* here was a master at tormenting her brothers. She let me in on some truly diabolical ways to turn spoiled cat food into a major problem. Little by little, I suspected she might have been the one that stunk out her own school by somehow getting it into the ventilation system. I even tried it on a small scale at my house last week, and everybody had to stay at a hotel. Except me, I stayed at Jamie's.

"The other day at lunch when *Colette* said how easy it would be to shut down a school, I knew it was her."

And when it's spoiled — CAT FOOD — it's even worse

"YOU SHUT DOWN A SCHOOL????" I said, horrified. Angeline was just as stunned.

"The smell wasn't supposed to last that long. I used too much cat food. It was too spoiled. But it wasn't dangerous. Just stinky."

"WHY???" Angeline asked. "Why did you do it?"

But Isabella wasn't done talking. "It was because she didn't want to do the school voting here at Wodehouse, I think. But I still don't know why."

Isabella reminded me of one of those lawyers you click past on TV when you're trying to find something worth watching.

Colette's voice got real low and she told us that one time at school her friend made her laugh while she was eating lunch, and she shot spaghetti out of her nose, and the teachers were afraid it was an intestine or a vein or something, so the school nurse had to come down to the lunchroom and remove it while the entire world of her school watched.

OMG

After that, she was up all night crying, and was so tired the next day that she fell asleep in class with a permanent marker in her mouth and it leaked and left a blue spot on her tongue that still hasn't come off. She said there were a bunch of other things like that, and because of them, she doesn't have any friends, and she never wins anything in the voting.

Can you believe it???? *Colette* IS "that girl from another school" who we've heard so much about!

"Wodehouse isn't a bad school," she said. "In fact, there's nothing wrong with here except it's where I'm from. Sorry I screwed up your voting. I just wanted to win **PRETTIEST** for once."

"But how did you know when we were doing the voting at our school?" I asked.

"A good friend of my mom's has a son at your school. It just came up in conversation," *Colette* said.

"What's his name?"

Colette shrugged her shoulders. "I don't know. I don't even know his mom's name. I just call her **T.U.L.W.N.I.F.** It stands for **That Ugly Lady Whose Name I Forget**."

We told her we were almost sure we knew the kid.

Isabella pulled the ballots from her backpack. "*Colette*, you didn't win **PRETTIEST**. Blondwad here figured out a way to beat you," Isabella said.

"I won **MOST CLEVER**," she added, "but I don't want it if I don't deserve it. You probably deserve it more than me."

It was strange to hear Isabella say that she didn't want something that she didn't deserve. That's usually exactly what she wants most. And now I understand why Isabella wanted to control the voting: not so she could cheat, but so nobody could cheat her. **She's soooooo suspicious.**

And I think that *Colette* was especially intriguing to Isabella. She had never met anybody who knew as much about getting even with mean brothers.

Isabella *respected Colette,* and I'm not sure Isabella has ever felt respect for another human being before. It weirded me out a little to see it.

Then *Colette* said, "But *Angeline* outsmarted me. And *you* figured it out. I hardly think that makes *me* most clever."

Isabella said she knew what to do, and we all promised to go along with it. We all knew what that meant.

"BROKE A PROMISE TO ISABELLA" is something we could all easily imagine on our tombstones.

Friday 27

Dear Dumb Diary,

Isabella revealed the results of the vote in school today. Angeline and I were there. We were only interested in a couple of categories, and we watched as Isabella posted them one at a time on the bulletin board outside the office.

Sally won for **MOST CLEVER.** Not Angeline, not *Colette*, and not Isabella. Sally is really smart, and that's a lot like clever.

IN BLOND SUSPENSE

THE VOTES ARE IN

MOST CLEVER
SALLY

Margaret won for **MOST ARTISTIC,** and she smiled so hard that her ugliness magically vanished. Like I said, her little chewed-pencil sculptures are grossly impressive. Isabella whispered to us that I really got the most votes, but I can't win in two categories. Plus, she said, I almost won for **FUNNIEST,** which I never would have expected.

BEFORE
(ugly)

AFTER
(less ugly)

Amazing what a smile CAN DO for YOUR LOOKS. AND SPITTING OUT YOUR SLOBBERY GROSS PENCIL.

I didn't even see my name until Isabella posted the one for **BEST FRIENDS: JAMIE, ANGELINE, ISABELLA.**

We looked at Isabella for the explanation, even though Angeline was making such high little squeals, I just knew that not only could she easily make a dog pee if one was here, but if she didn't stop soon, we were in danger of Margaret—who was a bit overexcited—letting loose.

A BLOND GIRL'S SQUEAL IS 80% HIGHER-PITCHED THAN A HUMAN'S.

Isabella took a deep breath before she explained herself.

"I didn't have a lot of options," she began. "We all deserve to win SOMETHING. We all had the votes to get SOME kind of prize.

"Officially, Angeline did win for PRETTIEST. But she kind of cheated, and the way she cheated could have gotten her the prize for MOST CLEVER, even though I got the votes for it. So, what else could I do? *Colette* probably deserved it most, but she didn't get the votes."

Isabella reached into her backpack and pulled out a card. "*This* is why we're BEST FRIENDS." Isabella posted the card for PRETTIEST. It said *Colette*.

"It doesn't mean exactly that we're *each other's* best friends, but we are, for sure, the best friends that *Colette* has . . . for now."

Isabella had really come through for a foreigner. I guess it was because she got to *know Colette*.

"They'll hear about this over at Wodehouse Middle School," Angeline said. "Things will change for *Colette*. You're right, Isabella: We *are Colette's* best friends." Angeline knows what she's talking about, of course. It's hard to imagine a bigger expert on the effects of prettiness.

"But best of all," Angeline giggled, "is that I'm **NOT THE PRETTIEST THIS YEAR!**" And she squealed and squirmed and jumped up and down.

"But I am a **BEST FRIEND!!!!** And that's *something!*" Angeline squeaked and then nearly floored us with the smothering beauty of her **HUGE SMILE.** Winning for something other than **PRETTIEST** was the best thing she could have hoped for, and kind of what I was hoping for her, too.

ANGELINE'S AWESOMEST SMILE CANNOT BE DRAWN BY THE HUMAN HAND.

"But just out of curiosity," I said to Angeline. "How could you be so sure that *I* wouldn't win for prettiest?"

Angeline laughed a little. "Well, for one thing, there's that voice you've been doing."

"You mean my Italian accent?"

Then Angeline *really* laughed. "That's not an Italian accent. I speak Italian," she said. "My Italian tutor has an Italian accent."

I turned to Isabella, who just shrugged.

"Wait a second. Your grandma doesn't have an Italian accent?" I asked.

GRAMMA
JACK
-O-
LANTERN?

"Not exactly," Isabella said. "She was born three miles from here. She talks like that because her dentures are broken, and she's too cheap to get them fixed. They're held together with tape—Hey!—I'll bet that's why you almost won for **FUNNIEST**. You said you wanted an accent. I figured a speech impediment was about the same thing."

It's true. Isabella doesn't like people from other places. She *does* think of accents as speech impediments.

Be thankful you are not tippy-toed and prissy

Isabella considers Ballet just a complicated Limp.

She says it's caused by those HORSE-LIKE thighs.

I was just getting ready to let Isabella have it when Aunt Carol limped out of the office to read the names on the bulletin board. She saw the three of us listed as best friends and gave us a giant four-way hug. "This is so perfect," she said. Then she pulled us into the office, where she gave us each a beautifully wrapped present. Assistant Principal Devon (Angeline's uncle and Aunt Carol's loverboy) was standing there, grinning.

my future uncle

my current aunt

Aunt Carol was a little weepy-eyed. "Jamie, you're my favorite niece, and Angeline, after your uncle and I get married, I just know you're going to be my other favorite niece. Isabella, you're best friends with both of my favorite nieces, which makes you a best friend of mine. And without your expert advice, I just know my wedding wouldn't be what it should be."

Aunt Carol was so emotional, for a second I was sure she was going to tell us she had some sort of horrible disease. But it turned out to be much worse.

She said, "Girls, I want you to be my bridesmaids." Angeline's squeals got even higher and louder, and I saw Margaret run down the hall. Leave it to Angeline to figure out a way to pee somebody else's pants for them.

And I just know at THAT EXACT MOMENT, somewhere in FARAWAY WHERETHEHECKISTAN, Angeline's piercing SQUEAL ALSO MADE A DOG AS GROSS AS MARGARET

Then we opened our presents. **They were clogs.** Aunt Carol said she couldn't find any so-called bridal clogs, but she's sure these are close enough, and if we wear them a little bit every day, our feet should stop bleeding by the wedding.

As we tried them on, it got worse. Aunt Carol brought out a sketch made by her dressmaker. It was of our bridesmaid gowns. You guessed it: They were brown and poofy. **Very very poofy.**

poofy

even
poofier

poofiest

Cloggy

poof to the
EXTREME

the
poof
the
poof
the poof
is on fire

Saturday 28

Dear Dumb Diary,

Isabella offered to make Aunt Carol and Assistant Principal Devon break off their engagement so we don't have to wear the clogs. She was sure that she could make it happen in about a week.

I told her that was sweet, but I thought we'd gotten ourselves into this and now we'd have to live with it.

Angeline gave us **B.F.F.** necklaces.

Isabella says that they kind of prove that we own Angeline a little bit, like a dog tag proves you own your dog. Isabella says it will magically increase our popularity and she seemed so happy about that that I'm wondering if she had considered that when she made us all **BEST FRIENDS**. (Would Isabella ever actually **DO** something like that?)

What she said about the dog tag made sense to me, so I gave my **B.F.F.** necklace to Stinker. I'll have to figure out what to tell Angeline when she comes over to finish that assignment that I knew all along was going to get put off until the day before it was due.

I'm not trying to force Stinker to learn any more foreign languages. I realize he already speaks one: **DOG**. And I think I have a new opinion about other people in other places anyway.

I got an e-mail from *Colette*. Here it is:

Dear Jamie —

I told the principal what I did with the cat food and why, and I'm getting punished, but they're going easy on me because I confessed.

The PRETTIEST award I won at your school made a big difference for me here. I didn't eat lunch alone today, and nobody called me Collie all day. Mackerel Middle School is the best school in the world. You guys are super nice!

Luv,

Colette

PS: You'll like this. Today at lunch, one of my friends told me that she heard about this girl at some other school, who was going around talking like she had a speech impediment or something, and when the principal found out, he made her wear wooden shoes. Can you believe it?

So I'm their "girl at some other school"!!!

I guess every place is somebody else's **Best Place On Earth**, and somebody else's **Worst Place On Earth** at the same time.

And if you ignore the **parsley** garnish, deep down, we're all sliced from the same meat loaf.

I suppose there's nothing wrong with where I am except that now as far as the Whole World of My School is concerned, Angeline and Isabella and I are **BEST FRIENDS;** the **BROWNEST, POOFIEST, CLOGGIEST** best friends in school.

Thanks for listening, Dumb Diary.
See you at the wedding!

Jamie Kelly

PS: And let's see you pretty your way out of **THIS** outfit, Angeline.

MWAH
HAH
HAH
HAH